Published by Checkerboard Press, Inc., 30 Vesey Street,
New York, New York 10007

MUDPIE, KITT'NVILLE, KITT'NS, and character names
are trademarks of Guy Gilchrist Productions, Inc.

ISBN: 1-56288-091-8 Library of Congress Catalog Card Number: 91-8203
Printed in the United States of America   (F1/10)   0 9 8 7 6 5 4 3 2

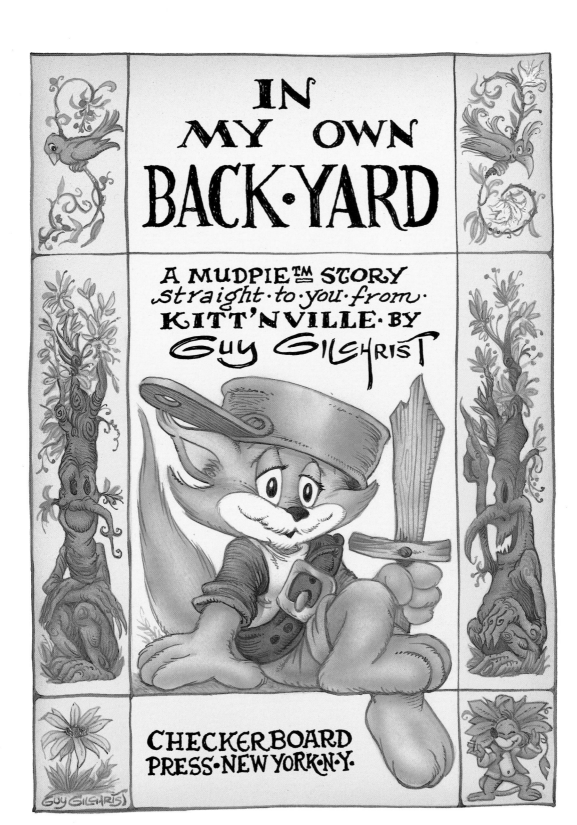

My name is Mudpie, and this is a story about how I use my imagination. When I make up a story, play make-believe, or draw a picture, that's using imagination.

My favorite place to imagine things
is right in my own backyard.

Today I imagine that I am a jungle guide in Africa.

Look! There's a lion running across the plains! There's an elephant! There's a rhinoceros!

There is the world-famous explorer! "Dr. Banjoey, I presume?"

We explore the jungle together,
right in my own backyard.

I'm a cowboy kitt'n riding through the desert in the Old West.

"How-de-do, Sheriff Pawdette."
We camp near a tall cactus . . . that grows in my own backyard.

I'm Captain Kitt'n, the brave, courageous superhero!

I protect the world from bad guys, right in my own backyard.

10 . . . 9 . . . 8 . . . 7 . . . 6 . . . 5 . . . 4 . . . 3 . . . 2 . . . 1 . . .
Blastoff! Spacekitt'n Mudpie heads to Mars.

I'm floating in my spacecraft . . . right in my own backyard.

I'm Sir Mudpie, knight of Kitt'nville. I duel with the cruel black knight . . .

and free the fair maiden locked in the castle tower.

Sir Mudpie and the fair maiden jump onto the back of a friendly dragon. I shout, "Dragon! Take me home!" And do you know what? That's just where the dragon takes me . . .

 home to my own backyard.